Date: 1/19/12

E WILLSON
Willson, Sarah.
Dora's backpack /

Dora's Backpack

adapted by Sarah Willson
based on the teleplay by Eric Weiner
illustrated by Robert Roper

Simon Spotlight/Nick Jr.

New York   London   Toronto   Sydney   Singapore

Visit us at www.abdopub.com

Library bound edition © 2006

Spotlight, a division of ABDO Publishing Company, is a school and library distributor of high quality reinforced library bound editions.

SIMON SPOTLIGHT

An Imprint of Simon & Schuster Children's Publishing Division
1230 Avenue of the Americas, New York, New York 10020

ISBN 0-689-84720-3

ISBN 1-59961-070-1 (Reinforced library bound edition)

All Spotlight books are reinforced library binding and manufactured in the United States of America.

¡Hola! I'm Dora, and this is my friend Backpack! I need to return eight books to the library, and Backpack's going to help me. We have to get there before it closes. Will you help us too?

Great! First we need to find Boots the monkey. Do you see him?

Now we have to find the quickest way to the library. Who do we ask for help when we don't know which way to go? The Map! There's a map inside my Backpack. Say, "Map!"

The Map says we have to go over the Troll Bridge and then cross Turtle River. That's how we'll get to the Library.

We made it to the Troll Bridge, but the Grumpy Old Troll won't let us cross unless we solve his riddle. Can you help us solve it?

"Here is one of my hardest quizzers," says the Grumpy Old Troll. "To cut through the net, use a pair of . . ."
What do you think the answer is?

Scissors! That's right. Can you find a pair of scissors in my Backpack? We need them to cut through the net.

We did it! We made it over the Troll Bridge. So next comes Turtle River, but there's a storm cloud! It's going to rain!

Can you see if Backpack has something to keep us dry?

You found the umbrella!
Oh, no! That storm cloud made the ground
all wet. Now Boots is stuck in the Icky-Sticky Sand.

Let's check Backpack for something to help Boots. Can you find it?

Right, a rope! I need your help to pull Boots out. Use your hands and pull, pull, pull! Great job!

Now we need to take that boat across Turtle River. Before we get into the boat what should we wear to be safe? Check Backpack!

Right! Life jackets! Uh-oh. I hear Swiper the fox. He's trying to swipe them! If you see him, say, "Swiper, no swiping!"

Thanks for helping us stop Swiper. Now we can cross Turtle River. We're almost at the library. Can you see it?

Here we are at the library.

Oh, no! The door is closed, but we can use Spanish to open it. If you say, *"abre,"* the door will open. Can you say, *"abre"*?

We did it! Now we can return my library books on time.

Can you count to make sure Val the librarian has all eight books from Backpack?

Hooray for Backpack! We couldn't have done it without her or you! Thanks for helping!